Snacking

Brushing

Dressing

Reading

Our Bedtime Tour

Taping

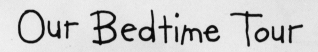

Fishing

Ant

Waiting

Goofing

Boating

Duck

To our friends,
EVELYN and SAM!
XXOO!!
Peggy Rathmann
2020

10 Minutes till Bedtime

PEGGY RATHMANN

G. P. PUTNAM'S SONS · NEW YORK

Published simultaneously in Canada. Manufactured in China by RR Donnelley Asia Printing Solutions Ltd.
Lettering by David Gatti. Library of Congress Cataloging-in-Publication Data
Rathmann, Peggy. 10 minutes till bedtime / Peggy Rathmann.   p. cm.
Summary: A boy's hamster leads an increasingly large group of hamsters on a tour of
the boy's house, while his father counts down the minutes to bedtime. [1. Hamsters—Fiction.
2. Bedtime—Fiction.] I. Title. PZ7.R1936Te 1998 [E]—dc21 97-51295 CIP AC
ISBN 978-0-399-23103-2
16 17 18 19 20

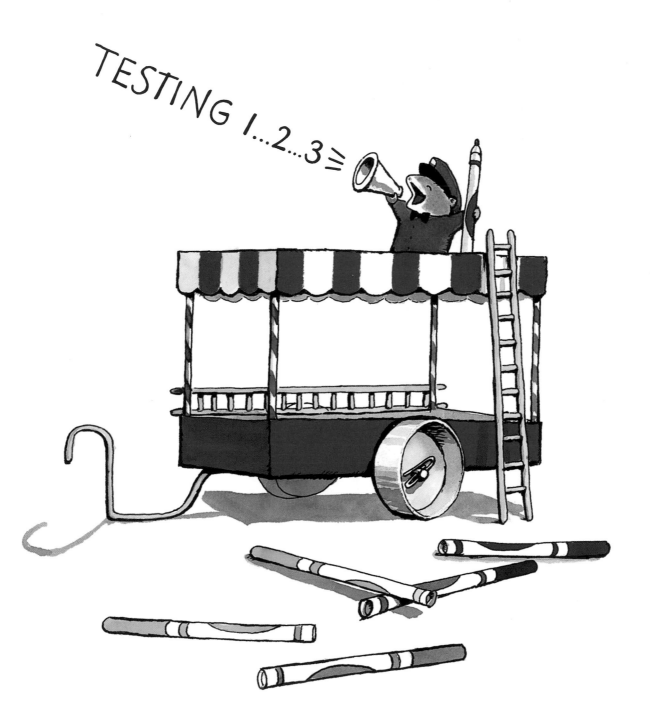

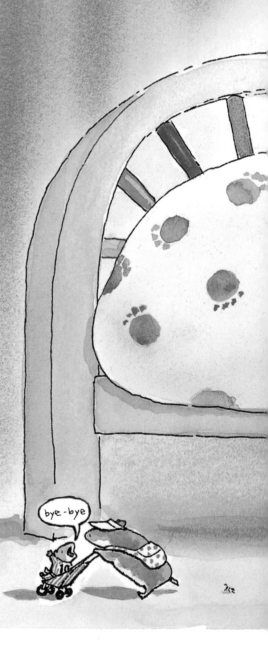